# THE AMERICAN

17  74

FELICITY, a spunky, spritely colonial girl,
full of energy and independence

18  24

JOSEFINA, an Hispanic girl whose heart and
hopes are as big as the New Mexico sky

18  54

KIRSTEN, a pioneer girl of strength and
spirit who settles on the frontier

18  64

ADDY, a courageous girl determined to be
free in the midst of the Civil War

19  04

SAMANTHA, a bright Victorian beauty, an
orphan raised by her wealthy grandmother

19  34

KIT, a clever, resourceful girl facing the
Great Depression with spirit and determination

19  44

MOLLY, who schemes and dreams on the
home front during World War Two

# 1934
# KIT'S SURPRISE
## *A Christmas Story*

BY VALERIE TRIPP

ILLUSTRATIONS WALTER RANE

VIGNETTES SUSAN MCALILEY

American Girl ™

SCHOLASTIC INC.

New York  Toronto  London  Auckland  Sydney
Mexico City  New Delhi  Hong Kong  Buenos Aires

ISBN 0-439-39584-4

12 11 10 9 8 7 6 5 4 3 2         3 4 5 6 7/0

Printed in the U.S.A.                23

First Scholastic printing, November 2002

PICTURE CREDITS

The following individuals and organizations have generously given permission to reprint images contained in "Looking Back": pp. 68–69—© CORBIS (Hooverville Christmas, window); courtesy Jane Geving (ornaments); courtesy J. C. Allen & Son, Inc. (dinner); pp. 70–71—courtesy Jane Geving (pin); courtesy J. C. Allen & Son, Inc. (Santa Claus and girl); © CORBIS (store window); reprinted with permission from Montgomery Ward (aviator caps); pp. 72–73—courtesy J. C. Allen & Son, Inc. (gifts for needy children); © Minnesota Historical Society/CORBIS (distribution of Christmas baskets).

Edited by Tamara England and Judith Woodburn
Designed by Will Capellaro, Myland McRevey, Ingrid Slamer, and Jane S. Varda
Art Directed by Laura Moberly and Ingrid Slamer
Cover Background by Mike Wimmer

FOR GRETCHEN CRYER AND NANCY FORD
WITH THANKS

# TABLE OF CONTENTS

KIT'S FAMILY
AND FRIENDS

DAD
*Kit's father, a
businessman facing
the problems of the
Great Depression.*

MOTHER
*Kit's mother, who takes
care of her family and
their home with strength
and determination.*

KIT
*A clever, resourceful
girl who helps her family
cope with the dark days
of the Depression.*

CHARLIE
*Kit's affectionate
and supportive
older brother.*

UNCLE
HENDRICK
*Mother's wealthy and
disapproving uncle.*

MRS. HOWARD
*Mother's garden club
friend, who is a guest in
the Kittredge home.*

STIRLING
HOWARD
*Mrs. Howard's son,
whose delicate health
hides surprising
strengths.*

RUTHIE
SMITHENS
*Kit's best friend, who
is loyal, understanding,
and generous.*

# CHAPTER ONE

# RICKRACK

On a bright, brisk Saturday afternoon in December, Kit Kittredge and her best friend Ruthie were cheerfully skittering down the sidewalk together like blown leaves. They were going to the movies, which they loved to do. When the girls were close to the movie theater, Kit leaned forward. She put her fists in her pockets and pushed down so that the front of her coat covered more of her dress.

"Hey, Kit, are you okay?" asked Ruthie kindly. "Does your stomach hurt or something?"

"No," said Kit. "I'm fine."

"Then how come you're all hunched over like that?" asked Ruthie.

"Because," said Kit, "I don't want everyone to see the rickrack on my dress."

"Why not?" asked Ruthie. "It's cute."

"Cute?" said Kit. "I hate it! My mother sewed it over the crease that was left when she let the hem down. I think it looks terrible!" Actually, Kit felt as if the rickrack were a big, embarrassing sign that said to everyone, *Look at this old outgrown dress I have to wear because I'm too poor to get a new one!* But she did not explain that to Ruthie.

Luckily, Ruthie was the kind of friend who was helpful even without explanations. "Walk behind me," she said. "I'll cover you up. Once we're inside the movie theater, it'll be dark and no one will see."

"Okay," said Kit. She scooched up behind Ruthie and the girls went into the theater. It was very warm inside. The air was buttery with the aroma of hot popcorn. And of course Ruthie was right—it *was* dark. Even so, when Kit sat down, she spread her coat over her lap to hide the rickrack.

"Want some?" asked Ruthie, generously holding out her popcorn to Kit.

"Thanks," said Kit. She took just two pieces of popcorn so that Ruthie wouldn't think she was a moocher. She already felt prickles of guilt because Ruthie had paid for her movie ticket.

Kit's father had lost his job five months ago because of the Depression. Her family didn't have money to spare for luxuries like new dresses or movie tickets. Kit didn't see how she'd ever be able to pay Ruthie back. Not that Ruthie expected her to! It just made Kit feel funny to owe money, even to her best friend. Kit squirmed in her seat. It never used to be awkward like this before Dad lost his job. Back then, Kit could pay her fair share. Maybe she shouldn't have agreed today when Ruthie, whose father still had his job at the bank, insisted on paying for her ticket. "Think of it as an early Christmas present," Ruthie had said. *Maybe I shouldn't have given in*, thought Kit.

But as soon as the newsreel began, Kit was very glad she had given in. Because there on the screen, smiling and waving at her, was Kit's absolute heroine—Amelia Earhart! Kit sat on the edge of her seat. The newsreel narrator was saying that Amelia Earhart was the first woman in history to fly a plane across the Atlantic Ocean all by herself. Kit knew everything about that daring solo flight. In fact, Kit had a newspaper article about it tacked to the wall above her desk at home. She'd read it a million times and stared at the photo of Amelia Earhart grinning her cocky, confident grin.

Now Kit stared at the movie screen as Amelia Earhart, in a sporty jacket, flight cap, and gloves, saluted the camera and climbed into the cockpit of her plane. Kit listened to the rumble of the plane's motor. She could almost feel the little plane straining to go faster, faster, faster as Amelia Earhart drove it down the runway. Then at last, she could feel the exhilaration of lifting up off the ground and soaring above the clouds!

The newsreel ended and Kit sank back. But she was so carried away by Amelia Earhart that the cartoon after the newsreel went by her in a blur. When the feature movie began, Kit didn't even try to make sense of the story. It was about a silly woman in a tiara singing and dancing her way up a staircase shaped like a wedding cake.

When at last the movie was over, Kit walked out into the late afternoon sunshine still thinking about Amelia Earhart. She

4

ignored the rickrack on her skirt hanging out below
her old winter coat. Amelia Earhart wouldn't let a
thing like that bother *her*.

Ruthie didn't mention the rickrack, either. She
turned to Kit and said, "Wasn't she wonderful?"

"Yes!" Kit agreed with enthusiasm. "Thank you
so much for bringing me today, Ruthie. I loved
watching her climb into that plane, and . . ."

"Not Amelia Earhart," Ruthie laughed. "I meant
Dottie Drew, the movie star!"

"Oh, *her!*" said Kit.

"Wasn't she beautiful?" breathed Ruthie. "Like a
princess almost."

"Uh, sure!" said Kit. Ruthie had a fascination for
movie stars and princesses, which quite frankly, Kit
did not share. But she didn't want to be rude. Ruthie
had paid for her ticket, after all. Kit might seem
ungrateful if she said she thought the woman in the
movie was silly.

But Ruthie knew Kit too well to be fooled. She
grinned. "I bet you didn't notice Dottie Drew at all,"
she said. "I should have known you'd care more
about Amelia Earhart. How come you're so crazy
about her?"

"She's smart," said Kit. "She's brave, too. When she makes up her mind to do something, she doesn't let anything stop her. She flew her plane across the ocean all by herself! She didn't need help from anybody." Kit spoke with determination. "I want to be like her."

"I know just what you mean," said Ruthie. "It's the same with me." She sighed. "I love to imagine that I'm a movie star or a princess."

Kit didn't think her serious ambitions were the same as Ruthie's starry-eyed daydreams at all. "That's different, Ruthie," she said. "First of all, Amelia Earhart's a real person who does real things that really matter. Movie stars and princesses are only phony glitter and glamour. And I don't imagine that I *am* Amelia Earhart. I want to be *like* her. Imagining that you're a princess is just make-believe."

"So?" Ruthie shrugged. "There's nothing wrong with make-believe."

"Maybe not," said Kit. "But imaginary stuff doesn't solve any problems or help anything."

"Oh, I think it does," said Ruthie. "Make-believe can take your mind off your troubles for a while. That's a help."

On the sidewalk ahead of the girls, Kit saw a sad
sight. It was a pile of household goods dumped on
the curb. A bed frame leaned against a chair, and a
lamp lay sideways on the ground. Books, clothes,
and pots and pans were jumbled together in a heap.
"Look," Kit said to Ruthie, pointing to the pile. "That
stuff belongs to a family that's been evicted. They've
been thrown out of their house because they can't
pay for it anymore. You've got to admit that make-
believe and imagination are not going to help *them*."

"They should've imagined a way to get money,"
Ruthie said. "They could've done *something*."

"I'm sure they tried," said Kit, thinking of how hard her own family struggled to pay the bills every month. "Maybe they just couldn't keep up."

"Then," said Ruthie, "they should have asked their friends for help."

"Maybe they were too proud to do that," said Kit.

Ruthie shook her head sadly. "And look where their pride got them—thrown out on the street," she said. "It won't be a very merry Christmas for their family, will it?"

"No," said Kit. "It won't." She shivered. "Come on," she said to Ruthie. "Let's run. It'll warm us up."

"Last one home is a rotten egg!" said Ruthie.

The girls ran the rest of the way to Kit's house. Kit's family had turned their home into a boarding house in order to earn some money after her dad lost his job. The boarders paid a weekly rent for their rooms and their meals. There were five boarders living in the house now: Mrs. Howard and her son Stirling, Mr. Peck, Miss Hart, and Miss Finney. Mr. Kittredge and Kit's older brother Charlie were fixing up another room so they could take in two more boarders as soon as possible. Kit was expected to do her share of the housework and to help with breakfast and dinner. So she quickly helped her mother scrub potatoes and put them in the oven before she and Ruthie went upstairs.

The girls were engaged in a secret project with Miss Hart and Miss Finney, two young nurses who rented what used to be the guest room. Miss Hart and Miss Finney had helped the girls unravel old sweaters and then use the wool to knit scarves. The scarves were almost finished, except for the fringe. Kit and Ruthie planned to give their scarves to their fathers for Christmas. Miss Hart planned to give hers to her boyfriend. Miss Finney said she wasn't sure which lucky guy would get her scarf. She couldn't decide between Tarzan and Franklin Roosevelt, who had just been elected president.

"Any news from Miss Hart's boyfriend lately?" asked Ruthie as the girls walked down the hall.

"Yup," said Kit. "He's coming to Cincinnati at Christmastime."

Miss Hart's boyfriend lived in Boston and sent her long letters in fat envelopes nearly every day. Miss Hart wrote back just as often, and her letters were just as long. Kit and Ruthie were both curious about the letters, and Ruthie especially liked to keep an eye on the progress of Miss Hart's romance.

"Miss Hart must be thrilled," said Ruthie. "Oh, if only they could have a romantic date while he's here! He'd probably ask her to marry him!"

"Miss Hart's boyfriend is a student in medical school," said Kit. "It'll take all his money to travel here. I don't think he'll have any left over for a fancy date."

"I wish he would," said Ruthie dreamily. "Miss Finney and Mr. Peck could go, too, and *they'd* fall in love. That's what would happen if they were in a movie."

"Well," said Kit crisply. "They're not in a movie. They're in real life."

"Too bad," sighed Ruthie.

Kit knocked on the door to Miss Hart and Miss Finney's room. There was no answer. "I guess they're working the weekend shift at the hospital," Kit said. "We won't be able to finish our scarves today. Want to go up to my room and make a newspaper instead?"

"Sure!" said Ruthie with enthusiasm.

Both girls loved making newspapers, which

they shared with the boarders and Kit's family. "We'll write about Amelia Earhart," said Kit.

"And Dottie Drew!" insisted Ruthie.

Kit pretended to be puzzled. "Who's she?" she asked.

"Very funny," said Ruthie.

"Okay," said Kit, grinning. "Her, too." And she danced up the attic stairs to her room the way Dottie Drew had danced up the wedding cake in the movie.

Ruthie leaned over Kit's shoulder. Kit was typing a paragraph Ruthie had written about Dottie Drew. "Wait a minute," Ruthie said. "It's Dottie Drew, not Duttio Drow. And she's a movie star, not a muvio tar. You better fix those mistakes."

"I can't," sighed Kit. "My typewriter keys are broken. The **o** looks like a **u** and the **e** looks like an **o** and the **s** doesn't work at all."

"Oh, well, that's okay," said Ruthie. She grinned, then said slowly, "I mean . . . uh, woll. That ukay."

Kit grinned, too. "I guess people will figure it out," she said. "Anyway, the pictures are great."

The girls had had the smart idea of asking Stirling to draw sketches of Amelia Earhart and Dottie Drew to illustrate their newspaper. Stirling was the same age as the girls, but he could draw as well as a grownup. "Stirling's a good artist," said Ruthie as she looked through his sketchpad. "See how he made Amelia Earhart look like you, Kit, freckles and all?"

Kit nodded. "And he put *you* in Dottie Drew's fancy ball gown and tiara," she said.

"That's me. Princess Ruthie," giggled Ruthie, striking a princessly pose.

Kit looked at the paper in her typewriter. "There's still a little space left," she said. "What should we write about?"

"Christmas!" said Ruthie. "We can say, 'Christmas is coming!' Everyone loves to read about that. I personally can't wait. I love everything about Christmas. What's your most favorite part, Kit?"

"Christmas Eve," said Kit. "That's when we put up our tree. Charlie's going to get us a free tree this year. We always decorate our tree on Christmas Eve. It looks so beautiful, especially the lights. We turn them on when we finish decorating, and we have dinner next to the tree. Mother always makes waffles. It's our tradition. I love it."

"I love the tradition that you and I have," said Ruthie, "when we go downtown with our mothers on the day after Christmas."

"Ruthie," Kit began, "I'm sorry. I'm afraid—"

But Ruthie talked over her. "I know you and your mother are awfully busy this year, what with the boarding house and all," she said. "So I was thinking that maybe this Christmas, instead of the whole day, we could go downtown just for a few hours instead. That'd be just as fun, wouldn't it?"

Kit believed in telling the truth, even when it was hard. "Time isn't the only problem, Ruthie," she said. "My mother and I don't have any money for lunch at a fancy restaurant or tickets to a show. We don't have money for presents even. Not this year."

"That's what I figured," said Ruthie. "So I thought we could change our tradition and just go window-shopping and have a winter picnic or something."

"I think," said Kit slowly, "it would wreck our tradition to change it."

"We wouldn't change *all* of it," said Ruthie. "We'd still get all dressed up in our best dresses, and—"

"I'd have to wear this rickrack dress," Kit cut in, "which I hate." She knew she sounded like a sourpuss, but she couldn't help it.

"But it's *Christmas*," Ruthie insisted. "You never know what might happen. You might get a new dress."

Kit shook her head. "The last thing I want my family to do this Christmas is to spend money on me," she said. "I don't want dresses or outings or presents. The only thing I want is to find a way to make money."

"Find a wicked ogre," said Ruthie. "Lots of times in fairy tales a princess is kind to an ogre, and then he spins straw into gold for her, or he enchants her so that jewels come out of her mouth when she talks, or he grants her three wishes."

Kit felt annoyed at Ruthie and her princesses. She and her family were real people, not characters in a fairy tale. "For Pete's sake!" she said. "It takes work, not wishes, to solve problems. That make-believe stuff is silly. There are no ogres in Cincinnati."

14

Ruthie just grinned. "Watch out," she said. "If you're not nice, the ogre makes snakes and toads come out of your mouth. How'd you like that?"

"Not much," said Kit. Impatiently, she pushed the silver arm that moved the paper up and out of the typewriter. But she pushed a little too hard, because, to her horror, it came off in her hand. "Oh no!" she cried, holding the silver arm up for Ruthie to see. "Look what I've done!"

"Uh-oh," said Ruthie. "Can you screw it back on?"

"No!" said Kit. "Oh, now the typewriter won't work at all!"

"Come on," said Ruthie, heading for the stairs. "Let's go get your dad. I bet he can fix it."

"I sure hope so," said Kit.

The two girls hurried downstairs. They paused in the hallway outside the living room because they heard Kit's parents talking to someone. The conversation sounded serious, so they knew they shouldn't barge in and interrupt.

Kit's dad was talking. "The room should be ready by the middle of January," he said. "Then we can take in two more boarders."

"I'm afraid that'll be too late," said the other voice. The girls looked at each other in surprise. It was Ruthie's dad, Mr. Smithens, speaking. Ruthie started to go into the room, but Kit held her back. "I've come today as a friend," Mr. Smithens said. "Your name is on a list of people who owe money to the bank, people who're behind on their mortgage payments. I came to warn you that if you can't catch up on your payments, the bank will take your house and you'll be evicted."

*Evicted!* Kit felt as if she'd been hit hard in the stomach.

"I'll hold off the bank until after the holidays," Ruthie's dad said. "But if you can borrow the money from someone, you should. Do you think your aunt in Kentucky might help, Jack? Or, Margaret, how about your uncle here in Cincinnati?"

Kit's mother started to answer, saying, "Well, I—"

"Thanks, Stan," Kit's dad interrupted. "We'll figure something out."

Kit could hardly breathe. Evicted! She and her family were going to be thrown out of their house! All of their belongings would be tossed out onto the sidewalk, just like those she and Ruthie had seen on

*"If you can't catch up on your payments, the bank will take your house and you'll be evicted," said Mr. Smithens.*

their way home from the movies. *It's going to happen to my family*, she thought. *It's going to happen to me.* She shuddered, and Ruthie touched her arm.

"Oh, Kit," Ruthie whispered. "What'll you do? I wish . . ."

*Wish!* thought Kit. She jerked her arm away. She couldn't bear to hear Ruthie say one of her silly things about wishes and princesses and make-believe. Not now. It was bad enough that Ruthie had been there to overhear the terrible, humiliating news! Without a word, Kit turned sharply and went back up the stairs to her room, leaving Ruthie all alone in the hall.

# THE BRIGHT
# RED DRESS

That night, after the last dinner dish was washed and dried, Mother took off her apron, put on her hat and coat, and went out. She didn't say where she was going, but Kit knew. Mother had a rich old relative named Uncle Hendrick who lived alone in a big, gloomy house near downtown Cincinnati. Kit knew Mother was going to ask Uncle Hendrick for money so that they wouldn't be evicted from their house.

Kit was reading in bed when Mother returned. When she came up to kiss Kit goodnight, Mother's face was tired.

"Uncle Hendrick said no, didn't he?" said Kit.

Mother was surprised. "How did—" she began.

"I heard Mr. Smithens talking to you and Dad," Kit said in her straightforward way. "I know about us being evicted. I figured you went to Uncle Hendrick to ask for money. And," Kit repeated, "he said no, didn't he?"

"I'm sorry, Kit," Mother said sadly. "It's not fair for a child to have to worry about such things." She sighed. "But you're right. Uncle Hendrick believes that money must be earned by hard work, not given away. He says we've been living beyond our means. He thinks it was foolish of us to buy this big house in the first place, and it would be throwing good money after bad to help us keep it. If we are evicted, he wants us to move in with him."

Kit sat bolt upright. "Oh, no!" she said. "We'd hate that! All the boarders would leave. It'd be awful."

Mother smiled a sad smile. "We may not have a choice," she said. "And we may lose the boarders anyway. At this point, we don't have enough money to pay even the electric bill. I don't think we can ask the boarders to stay if our electricity is cut off and we don't have any lights."

Kit couldn't bear to see Mother look so defeated. "I'll find a way to help, Mother," she said. "I promise

I will. I'll find a way to make money."

"Well," said Mother, "there is a way you can help, though I don't think it'll make any money."

"What is it?" asked Kit.

"Uncle Hendrick says he's ill," said Mother. "I think he's really just lonely and fretful. But he wants me to come back tomorrow and every day until he feels better. I'm so busy here, I don't see how I can. Would you do it? You could go tomorrow, and then next week you could go after school. During your Christmas vacation, you could go for a few hours every day. He needs someone to keep him company and do errands and walk his dog."

Kit's heart sank. Uncle Hendrick's old black Scottie dog, Inky, was the meanest, most hateful dog in Cincinnati. He was even meaner than Uncle Hendrick. And Uncle Hendrick was exactly like Ebenezer Scrooge in *A Christmas Carol* before the ghosts visited him and scared him into being nice. "I know it's a lot to ask," said Mother. "But it would be a great help to me."

"I'll do it," said Kit. This was her chance to help.

Mother hugged Kit. "That's my girl," she said,

and now her smile was real. "Thank you. Uncle Hendrick knows we don't have a car anymore. He gave me a nickel for the streetcar. I'll give it to you tomorrow. Now don't read too long. You need to rest. Good night!"

"Good night!" said Kit.

Mother went downstairs. Kit had read only a few pages when her brother Charlie appeared. "Hi," he said. "Mother told me what you're doing. I thought you could use this." He tossed an old tennis ball to Kit.

"What's this for?" she asked as she caught it.

"It's for stinky Inky to fetch," said Charlie. "Throw it really, *really* far."

Kit grinned. "Thanks, Charlie," she said.

Charlie grinned, too. "You're welcome," he said. "G'night, Squirt!"

"'Night, Charlie!" said Kit. She switched off her light and lay in the dark thinking, *Maybe Uncle Hendrick's won't be so bad after all.*

But it *was* bad. In fact, it was terrible.

The first bad thing that happened was that

Kit missed the streetcar. She had to run all the way to Uncle Hendrick's house because she was supposed to be there promptly at noon and Uncle Hendrick was a stickler for time. Luckily, Kit was a fast runner. But it was very cold, and Kit's nose was red and her hair was blown every which way by the time she got to Uncle Hendrick's door. She tried to catch her breath and straighten herself up a little. But Inky was barking wildly and scrabbling his claws against the other side of the door, so Uncle Hendrick opened it before she even knocked. That was the next bad thing.

"What are *you* doing here?" he bellowed over Inky's yapping.

"Mother's too busy," Kit bellowed back. "I'm here instead."

"I don't want *you*," said Uncle Hendrick. "Go away!"

Inky growled as if to echo Uncle Hendrick, then launched into another frenzy of barking.

Kit didn't budge. She'd promised Mother that she would help. It would take more than Uncle Hendrick's bluster and Inky's snarls to discourage her.

*"What are **you** doing here?" Uncle Hendrick bellowed over Inky's yapping.*

"Well, you're here, so you might as well stay," said Uncle Hendrick. "Hurry up! Come in! Don't stand there like a fool and let the heat out. It costs good money." Kit stepped inside, and he shut the door behind her. "If your family had paid more attention to how much things like heat cost, you wouldn't be in the state you're in now," he scolded. "Come with me."

"Yes, sir," said Kit. Now that the door was shut, she realized how dark it was inside Uncle Hendrick's house. The darkness seemed old somehow, and permanent, as if it had been there a long time and always would be there. Kit followed Uncle Hendrick and Inky upstairs to Uncle Hendrick's huge room. He sat down in the most comfortable chair by the coal fire and put a blanket over his knees. Inky jumped up into the other chair by the fire. He watched Kit's every move with his sharp, unfriendly black eyes.

Kit went to Uncle Hendrick to give him the nickel she hadn't used.

"What's that?" he snapped, peering at the coin.

25

"It's the nickel you gave Mother for the street-car," said Kit. "I didn't use it. I missed the streetcar, so I—"

"I don't care if you came on a winged chariot," Uncle Hendrick said, impatiently pushing her hand away. "You got here on time. That's all that matters."

"You mean I can keep the nickel?" asked Kit.

"Yes!" barked Uncle Hendrick, sounding a lot like Inky. "Now stop jabbering! Hand me my book! Not the red one, the brown one! And how am I supposed to read it? Hand me my eyeglasses, too, and be quick about it."

That's how it went all afternoon. Uncle Hendrick sat in his chair and ordered Kit downstairs to make him a cup of tea. When she brought it up, he ordered her downstairs again for the milk and sugar. He wanted her to open the drapes, then close them again, to move his chair closer to the fire and then farther away. He wanted his medicine. He wanted the newspaper. He wanted a pen and ink and writing paper, then a stamp.

It seemed to Kit that for an old man who was supposed to be sick, Uncle Hendrick certainly had plenty of energy for bossing her around and pointing out what she was doing wrong, which was everything. She filled the teacup too full and sloshed tea into the saucer. She wobbled the spoon when she poured the medicine into it. She pulled too hard on the cord that closed the drapes but didn't push hard enough when moving his chair. She talked too fast and walked too slow. There was no pleasing Uncle Hendrick.

Inky was just as bad. When it was time for his walk, Kit put her coat back on. She clipped Inky's leash onto his collar. "Come, Inky," she said. Inky didn't move. He growled deep in his throat and bared his teeth at her.

"You'll have to carry him," said Uncle Hendrick. "He doesn't like walking down the stairs."

Kit hoisted the fat old dog up in her arms and carried him down the stairs and out the door. Once his feet hit the sidewalk, Inky took off. He strained on the leash, practically pulling Kit's arm out of its socket. When they got to the park, Kit bent down to show Inky the tennis ball. "Look, Inky," she said. Then she threw the ball as hard as she could. "Go get it, Inky!" she said.

But Inky just sniffed, as if to say, "Why should I?" He lowered himself to the grass and refused to move. Kit had to fetch the ball herself, and then drag Inky back to Uncle Hendrick's house and carry him upstairs.

"You," she hissed, as she set him down, "are a horrible dog."

Inky's black eyes glittered. He looked pleased with himself. He jumped into his chair and promptly went to sleep.

Uncle Hendrick was asleep, too. So Kit had to sit perfectly still and wait for him to wake up. She amused herself by thinking of words to describe Uncle Hendrick and Inky. *They're both grouchy and grumpy,* she thought. *They're crabby, cranky, critical, and cross.*

When at last Uncle Hendrick woke up, he announced that it was time for Kit to go home. Kit put on her coat, which was now covered with Inky's black hair. "Good-bye," she said to Uncle Hendrick. "I'll see you tomorrow."

"Humph," said Uncle Hendrick. He didn't sound pleased or displeased. He reached into his pocket and pulled out two nickels. "Here," he said.

"One for the streetcar home and
one for the streetcar here tomorrow."

"But—" Kit began to say.

"Take them and go!" ordered Uncle Hendrick.
So she did.

When she closed the door behind her, Kit
took a deep breath. The cold, clean winter air
felt wonderful on her cheeks. It cleared the stuffy,
mediciney, doggy smell of Uncle Hendrick's house
out of her nose. As Kit walked to the streetcar
stop, she had an idea.

*I'll walk home*, she thought. *Uncle Hendrick
said he didn't care if I use the nickels for the streetcar
or not. I won't use them. I'll save them and give
them to Mother to help pay the electric bill. That
will be my Christmas surprise for her.*

The thought cheered Kit, and she turned up
her collar and started the long walk home with
determined steps. But it was awfully cold, and the
walk was all uphill. By the time Kit got to her own
house, she was tired and cold to the bone. She was
hungry, too. It was disheartening to know she had
missed Sunday dinner and there'd be only crackers
and milk for supper.

When Kit opened the front door, she was surprised to see Ruthie sitting on the bottom step in the front hall. Ruthie had a big white box on her lap. Her face was bright and eager. She looked as if she was struggling to hold a surprise inside and was about to burst. "Hi!" she said to Kit. "I thought you'd never get here!"

"Hi," said Kit as she wearily hung up her coat. "I don't think we can finish our scarves today, Ruthie. I have chores to do."

"Oh, I didn't come for that!" said Ruthie. She jumped up from the stair and thrust the big white box at Kit. "Here!" she said. "This is for you." Ruthie was so excited, she danced around Kit impatiently as Kit knelt down to open the box. "Wait till you see!" she said. "Now everything will be okay!"

Kit lifted the lid of the box. Inside, she saw a bright red dress. She took it out and held it up, puzzled. "But this is your dress, Ruthie," she said at last.

"It *was*," said Ruthie. "It's my last year's Christmas dress. It doesn't fit me anymore. I'm getting a new one, so I'm giving this one to you."

The bright red dress was *so* red it seemed to make Kit's hands warm just to hold it. Kit felt her face get warm, too, but the heat came from the burning sting of embarrassment. She was humiliated, not delighted, by Ruthie's hand-me-down present. *Now Ruthie thinks of me as a poor, pitiful beggar girl,* she thought. Kit swallowed. "Thanks," she managed to say politely. She tried very hard to smile.

"That's not all!" Ruthie burbled. "Look in the pocket! It's even better."

Kit reached into the pocket of the dress and pulled out four tickets to the ballet. There was also an invitation in Ruthie's handwriting that said:

*Mrs. Smithens and Ruthie Smithens*
*cordially invite*
*Mrs. Kittredge and Kit Kittredge*
*to a fancy tea at*
*Shillito's Restaurant*
*on December 26th*
*after the ballet*

31

"See?" said Ruthie, all aglow. "My mother bought the tickets, and she'll pay for the tea. Now we *can* have our special day. And you won't have to wear your rickrack dress."

Slowly, Kit slid the invitation and the tickets back into the pocket. She folded the dress carefully and put the lid back on the box. She stood up. "Thank you, Ruthie," she said stiffly. "But your dress is probably too big for me. And my mother and I are going to be busy on December 26th." She handed the big white box to Ruthie.

Ruthie looked at it, then at Kit. "What do you mean?" she asked.

"I have a job now," said Kit. "At my Uncle Hendrick's house."

"But you could take a day off," said Ruthie. "You could—"

"No," interrupted Kit coolly. "I couldn't. It's my responsibility." Ruthie's face looked so sad that Kit softened a bit. "Listen," she said. "I know you're just trying to be nice and generous, Ruthie. But don't you see? I can't wear your old dress."

"But my mother fixed it to fit you," said Ruthie. "And I thought you were embarrassed by the rickrack dress. I thought you hated it."

"I do hate it," said Kit. "But at least it's my own. I'd be embarrassed to wear your dress. And it's the same with the tickets and the tea. It would make my mother and me feel like sponges."

"Sponges?" asked Ruthie. Her voice sounded strained and tight.

"Yes," said Kit. "We'd be ashamed to let your mother pay for us."

"Ashamed!" said Ruthie, pink in the face and mad. "I think you should be ashamed of being so selfish. You're just only thinking of yourself! What about me? Did you ever stop to think that maybe you're ruining my Christmas with your stupid pride? You've got a houseful of people, and I'm all alone with just my mother and father. The most fun I ever have is with you. The day you and I spend together after Christmas is the very best part of Christmas for me. I thought you liked it, too. That's why my mother and I tried to fix it this year. But you're too stuck-up and stubborn to accept it. We were just trying to help."

"I don't want help," said Kit, bristling.

"Oh, I know!" said Ruthie. "You think you're

just like great old Amelia Earhart, flying all by herself without help from anybody."

Now Kit was mad, too. "At least I'm not so babyish that I think I'm a princess like you do," she said, the words lashing out as mean as snakes. "You're always talking about wishes and wicked ogres and make-believe. You don't know anything that's real. Your father still has his job. You can do whatever you want. You have everything, except you don't have any idea what the world is really like!"

"Well, now I know what *you* are really like," said Ruthie. "Mean."

"Well, you're spoiled," said Kit.

"Oh!" exclaimed Ruthie angrily. She grabbed her coat and went to the door. "I don't think we can be friends anymore."

"Good!" said Kit.

"Good-*bye*!" said Ruthie. Then she left, closing the door firmly behind her.

Kit stared at the door for a second, then turned and ran as fast as she could up the stairs to her room. She flung herself face-down on her bed. Oh, oh, *oh!* How could everything be so horrible? It wasn't *fair*. Her family had lost so much since Dad had lost his job. Not just money. They'd lost their feeling of being safe, their trust that things would work out for the best. They were probably going to lose their home. *And now I've lost the most important thing of all*, thought Kit. *My best friend.*

Kit buried her face in her pillow and cried.

CHAPTER
THREE

# THE WICKED
# OGRE

Kit couldn't allow herself to cry for long. She knew that all her afternoon chores were waiting for her. And Mother liked to give the kitchen floor a good scrub every Sunday night because there wasn't time during the week. Kit rolled over and sat up on her bed. She saw Amelia Earhart smiling at her from the newspaper photograph near her desk. *Come on, Kit,* Amelia seemed to say. *Gotta get up and go.* Even though she still felt miserable, Kit wiped her eyes, blew her nose, and went downstairs to the kitchen.

Mother had already put the chairs up on the kitchen table. She was filling a bucket with hot, soapy water at the sink. She turned to greet Kit

with a smile. But her smile faded when she saw
Kit's eyes, red from crying. "Oh, Kit, darling!" she
said. She dried her hands on her apron as she
hurried over to put her arm around Kit. "Was it that
bad at Uncle Hendrick's, then? He's so fussy. And
that awful what's-his-name, too. The Scottie dog!"

"Inky," Kit said. Mother smelled of soapsuds,
and Kit let herself lean against her. "He hates me."

"The way to that dog's heart is through his
stomach," said Mother. "I've got some cheese rinds in
the pantry. Even I can't figure out how to make them
edible. You can give them to Inky tomorrow when
you go there after school. That'll win him over."

"Thanks, Mother," said Kit, not very cheered.

"That's not all that's wrong, is it?" asked Mother.

"No," admitted Kit. "Ruthie and I had a fight."

"I see," said Mother. "What about?"

Kit poured out the whole story about Ruthie's
bright red dress, the ballet tickets, and the invitation
to tea. "It was wrong of me to say no for you, too,"
she said. "But I couldn't help it. I was just so *mad*."
Kit sighed. "It used to be easy to be friends with
Ruthie. It isn't anymore."

Mother nodded. "Your lives are very different

now," she said. "Things that are possible for Ruthie are not possible for you."

"The truth is," said Kit, "I'm jealous of her."

"And she," said Mother, "is jealous of you."

"Of me?" asked Kit, surprised. "But I'm the one who's lost everything. Why would she be jealous of me?"

"Oh, I don't know," said Mother. "I've had the impression that Ruthie envies you for having the boarders around, like a big, interesting family. It's awfully quiet at her house. And maybe she envies how your life is more grown-up now. People trust you to do important things."

"I never thought of it that way," said Kit, sighing. "All I know is that I'm sorry about the fight."

"I wish we could use the telephone," said Mother. The telephone had been turned off because they couldn't afford to pay the bill anymore. "Then you could call Ruthie and tell her that you're sorry. Well, you'll see her in school tomorrow. You can make it better then."

"Do you think so?" asked Kit hopefully.

"Of course!" said Mother. "It is never too late to repair a friendship." Mother lifted the pail of hot water out of the sink. "Let's scrub this floor now," she said. "I'm afraid it's never too late for that, either!"

❧

Mother was wrong. Kit was not able to patch things up with Ruthie the next day. Ruthie didn't stop to pick her up before school. And every time Kit tried to get Ruthie's attention during the morning, Ruthie turned away or hid herself in a group of girls. At lunchtime, in desperation, Kit wrote Ruthie a note and put it on her desk. She watched unhappily as Ruthie glanced at it, picked  it up in two fingers as if it were a dead toad, and tossed it, unopened and unread, into the wastepaper basket. Then Ruthie sashayed off to lunch with a bunch of girls who were in her dancing class. Kit used to be in the dancing class, too, but she'd had to drop out when her family couldn't afford *that* anymore, either.

Everyone at school noticed that Ruthie was shunning Kit. Stirling, who was actually pretty nice for a boy, tried to help. "Here," he said to Kit. "Give this to Ruthie." He handed Kit a picture he had drawn. The picture showed Kit flying an airplane like Amelia Earhart's. The passenger in the airplane was Ruthie dressed as a princess.

"Thanks, Stirling," Kit said. But she was afraid to give the drawing to Ruthie after what she'd said about princesses being babyish. So Kit put Stirling's drawing away in her book bag.

After three days of getting the cold shoulder, Kit gave up. It was clear that Ruthie was too mad to forgive her. She wouldn't even give Kit a chance to apologize. When Ruthie had said they couldn't be friends anymore, she'd meant it. School closed for vacation, and Kit and Ruthie still hadn't spoken.

Usually, Kit loved Christmas vacation because it meant she had more time to spend with her family and Ruthie. But this year, all it meant was that she had more time to spend with Uncle Hendrick and Inky. Uncle Hendrick still claimed he felt poorly, so every morning, after doing her chores at home, Kit went to his house. She walked there and back so she could save the streetcar fare. Her pile of nickels was growing. But that was the only good thing about going to Uncle Hendrick's house.

"Good gracious, you careless child! Don't use so much string!" Uncle Hendrick fussed at her one day as Kit was tying up a bundle of newspapers for him. "Do you think string grows on trees? I suppose you learned your wasteful ways from your spendthrift parents." He snorted. "They think that *money* grows on trees. Holes in their pockets, those two!"

Kit bit her lip to stop herself from saying to Uncle Hendrick, "That's not true!" He never missed a chance to be critical of her parents. He lectured her about how they deserved their poverty because they'd been extravagant and lived beyond their means. It made Kit furious. Sometimes she thought Uncle Hendrick was trying to make her mad on purpose so that she wouldn't come back. But Kit could be ornery, too. The meaner Uncle Hendrick was, the more determined she was not to give up. She wouldn't give him that satisfaction.

At the end of every day, Uncle Hendrick had errands for her to do on her way home. Every errand came with lots of fussbudgety instructions. "Take these shoes to be shined," Uncle Hendrick commanded one blustery day. "Here's a dime to pay for it." He shook his finger at Kit. "Tell the man that I demand good value for my money. The last time,

he left a scuff mark on the toe. Tell him don't think
I didn't see it."

"Yes, sir," said Kit. She put the shoes in her
book bag and the dime in her pocket.

"Leave these shirts at the laundry," said
Uncle Hendrick. "Tell them to put starch on the
collars and cuffs *only*. And tell them that I don't
want to see any buttons broken like the last time or
I'll deduct the cost of the buttons from their bill."

"Yes, sir," said Kit again. "Good-bye." She
gathered up the shirts, put on her coat, and left.

The laundry was closest, so Kit dropped off the
shirts first. Then she trudged along to the shoe-shine
shop. When she got there, a terrible sight met her
eyes. There was a big hand-lettered sign on the door:

Kit stood there in the bitter cold wondering
what to do. One thing was sure. Uncle Hendrick

would bite her head off and howl worse than Inky if she brought his shoes back unshined. So Kit took the shoes home. Using her dad's rags and polish, she shined them herself, rubbing until her arm ached. She carried the shoes back to Uncle Hendrick's house the next day, bracing herself for his persnickety words of criticism.

Before she could explain, Uncle Hendrick took the shoes from her. "There!" he said. "That's what I call a job well-done! Let that be a lesson to you, Kit. You only get your money's worth if you insist upon it."

Kit hid a smile. "Here's your dime back," she said. "The shop was closed. I shined the shoes."

"You?" said Uncle Hendrick. He studied the shoes again, then narrowed his eyes at her. "Then you earned the dime," he said brusquely. "Keep it."

Kit put the dime in her pocket. Then she faced Uncle Hendrick bravely. "Uncle Hendrick," she said. "I've been thinking. May I work for you? If I pick up your groceries, may I keep the tip you usually give the delivery man? If I deliver your letters, may I keep the cost of the stamps? And if I—"

"Stop!" shouted Uncle Hendrick. "You pester the life out of me! Get this straight once and for all, child. I don't care who does the work, as long as it's done to my satisfaction. You may keep any money you earn. Understand?"

"Yes, sir!" said Kit.

"Good!" said Uncle Hendrick. "Now don't bother me about this again."

That was all Kit needed to hear.

Starting then, whenever she could, Kit did Uncle Hendrick's jobs herself. She polished his shoes. She delivered his letters. She fetched his groceries. She brought him his newspaper. She washed his windows—and then washed them all over again because Uncle Hendrick said he saw streaks. Kit wanted to earn enough money to pay the electric bill, which she knew was about two dollars and thirty-five cents. Every day, she counted up the money she'd earned to see how close she was getting to her goal. Five days before Christmas Eve, Kit had one dollar and fifty-five cents. She needed eighty cents more. She knew she could earn ten cents a day by walking instead of riding the streetcar. That would be fifty cents. But it was going to be tough to earn the last thirty cents.

Still, Kit was determined, even though Uncle Hendrick's chores were hard. The winter streets were often slippery, and the winter darkness came earlier and earlier. But Kit kept saying to herself, *Think how surprised Mother will be when I give her the money I've earned.* The thought kept her going when the cold wind made her eyes water and slush seeped through her shoes and froze her feet. Sometimes Kit had to take dreadful old Inky with her when she did errands. He'd wind his leash around her legs and try to trip her, or roll in a puddle and then shake so that cold, dirty water splattered all over her. The *clink* of coins in her pocket helped Kit put up with Inky, and with Uncle Hendrick, too, even when he was at his most cantankerous.

There was one errand Kit liked to do even though it didn't earn her any money. Every few days, Uncle Hendrick sent her to the public library to return his books and pick up new ones the librarian set aside for him. The huge public library seemed like a hushed, warm heaven to Kit, filled as it was from floor to ceiling with books. Unfortunately, she never had time to linger there. Uncle Hendrick was always in a hurry to get his books, which seemed odd because they were so dull and boring they always put him to sleep.

It was during the afternoons while Uncle Hendrick dozed that Kit thought about Ruthie the most. She missed Ruthie. It would have been such a comfort to talk to her. She'd understand how hateful Inky was and how impossible Uncle Hendrick was.

One especially long afternoon, Kit sat watching Uncle Hendrick snore in his chair. One of his dull books had put him to sleep. Inky was contentedly tearing the cover off Charlie's tennis ball. Kit reached into her book bag, only to find that she'd left the book she wanted to read at home. Instead, she pulled out a pad of paper. It was Stirling's sketchpad, the one he'd used when he made sketches of Kit as Amelia Earhart and Ruthie as a princess. Kit looked at the sketches. Then, without planning to, she began to write.

*Once upon a time*, she began. And then the story seemed to sweep her away. It wasn't the kind of story she usually wrote for her newspaper.

*Once upon a time,* she began. And then the story
seemed to sweep her away.

This story was not about facts. It didn't report what was really happening. This story was about a completely different world, the kind of world Ruthie liked, a world that was imaginary. In this world, Kit could make anything she wanted to happen *happen.*

While she was writing, Kit forgot she was stuck in Uncle Hendrick's dreary house. She forgot about her family's money troubles, and the fact that the boarders might leave, and that her family might be evicted from their house. All that disappeared while she was in the world of her story.

When Uncle Hendrick woke up and blinked his eyes open, Kit felt herself snap back into the real world. It was as if she were waking up, too, from a wonderful dream. Kit hurriedly shoved the sketchpad back into her book bag, thinking, *Ruthie was right! Make-believe does make your troubles disappear for a while.* Kit wished she could tell Ruthie that she understood about make-believe now. Then Kit remembered that she and Ruthie weren't friends anymore. They weren't even speaking to each other.

After that first afternoon, Kit wrote more of her story every day. She began to look forward to her writing time, when the only sounds in the grim old house were Uncle Hendrick's snores, the hollow ticking of the clock on the mantle, and Inky's slobbery snuffles. Soon Kit began to see that writing made *all* of her day better. She thought about her story when she was outside doing errands, and it distracted her from the cold and her tired feet. She paid close attention to how things looked or smelled or sounded, trying to find just the right words to describe them for her story. When Uncle Hendrick woke up and fussed at her, it didn't bother her anymore. She listened carefully, in case she wanted to use anything he said in her story. Because Kit had discovered that Ruthie had been right about something else, too. There *was* a wicked ogre in Cincinnati: Uncle Hendrick.

# JEWELS

*Whooosh!*

A harsh wind blew sleet into Kit's face. She hunched her shoulders and wrapped her arms tightly around Uncle Hendrick's library books to keep them dry. It was Christmas Eve morning, and even a long list of errands and nasty weather could not dampen Kit's spirits. *I bet this sleet will turn into snow!* she thought. *How perfect! It'll be so cozy to have dinner next to the Christmas tree.*

Kit's family had not had time to put up their Christmas tree yet. But Kit was not worried. As soon as she was finished at Uncle Hendrick's this afternoon, she'd hurry home and help Dad and Charlie put up the tree and decorate it. Kit skipped with happiness, thinking of how surprised everyone would be when she gave Mother the money she had earned. Two dollars and forty cents—enough to pay the electric bill! She had earned the last thirty-five cents by selling Uncle Hendrick's rags to the ragman. *Now the boarders won't leave*, she thought. *Now we can light the Christmas tree lights and our tree will be as beautiful as every other year.*

Kit let herself into Uncle Hendrick's house. Inky barked at her as she climbed the stairs, and nipped at her feet as she went into Uncle Hendrick's room. "Stop that, Inky," said Kit. But the irritating dog would not settle down. He was restless all morning, prowling from window to window. Whenever the sleet clattered against the glass, sounding like a handful of thrown pebbles, Inky barked. Every once in a while, there'd be a loud *CRACK!* when a tree limb, weighted down by a heavy coating of ice, would snap. Inky howled whenever that happened.

When it was time for Inky's walk after lunch, the sleet still hadn't turned to snow. The dog stubbornly refused to go out, so Kit had to carry him, squirming and yowling, out the back door.

"Go ahead and yowl," she said to him. "Even you can't ruin this day for me, you horrible dog." She shivered as she waited for Inky to come back inside. It was bitterly cold, and the sleet showed no signs of stopping. Kit rubbed her arms with her hands. She tilted her head to look at the sky. It looked gray and hard, as if it, too, were encased in ice.

At last it was time for Kit to go home. She hurried into her coat and put her book bag on her back. She knew it was going to be a difficult and slippery walk home, and she was anxious to get started. "Good-bye," she said to Uncle Hendrick. "We'll see you tomorrow." Uncle Hendrick was much better, so he planned to take a cab to the Kittredges' house for Christmas Day.

"What? Oh! Yes, of course," said Uncle Hendrick. "Go along now. And close the door carefully behind you. I don't want it banging in this wind."

"Yes, sir!" said Kit. Joyfully, she pounded down the stairs and opened the door. A cruel blast of wind pushed so hard against her that she stumbled back. She bent her head forward, burying her chin in her collar, and pulled the door closed behind her. Ice slashed at her cheeks and stung her eyes. The streetlights were lit, and the street looked eerily beautiful. The tree branches were shiny with ice and glittered as if they were made of diamonds.

Kit took a step forward, and her feet flew out from under her. She landed hard on her bottom, so hard that she saw stars. Gingerly, Kit rolled to her hands and knees and tried to stand. She clutched at the iron railing that fenced Uncle Hendrick's yard, and inched her way forward to the sidewalk. It was slow going, and when the iron railing ended and there was nothing to hold on to, Kit fell again. This time she cracked her elbow so badly she winced with pain. Kit blinked back tears. She struggled to her feet again and tried to skate forward. But it was no use. For every step forward she managed to take, she seemed to slip backward twice as far. If she couldn't make any headway on the flat ground, there was no way she could get up the steep hill home, or even to the streetcar stop. Kit's coat was beaded with pearls of ice, and ice trickled down the back of her neck. Her feet were so numb they were heavy as lead. Sadly, Kit fought her way back to Uncle Hendrick's house and let herself inside.

"What are you doing here?" Uncle Hendrick snapped when he saw her.

"It's too slippery out," said Kit. "May I wait here till the sleet stops?"

Uncle Hendrick peered out the window. "It's not going to stop tonight," he announced, sounding pleased to give such bad news. "You'll have to stay the night."

"Oh *no!*" wailed Kit. "I can't. It's Christmas Eve. I *have* to get home."

"Don't be ridiculous!" barked Uncle Hendrick. "Stop whining! There's nothing to be done. You'll have to call your family and tell them you're staying here tonight."

"I can't," said Kit.

"Why not?" asked Uncle Hendrick impatiently.

"Our phone's not connected anymore," said Kit.

"Couldn't pay the bill, I suppose," said Uncle Hendrick sourly. "Typical! Well, then you'll have to call someone who can go to your house to tell your parents where you are. Call a neighbor or a friend."

A friend? Now Kit's heart felt as heavy and leaden as her feet. There was only one person she could call, and that was the last person on earth she wanted to call. But Kit had no choice. She went to the phone. Reluctantly, she made the call.

 *Maybe her mother will answer,* she thought.

But no. When the voice on the other end of the line said hello, Kit knew who it was right away.

"Ruthie?" she said. "It's me." Kit spoke all in a rush. "I know you're mad at me, but don't hang up. You don't have to talk to me. I wouldn't have called, but I'm stuck at my Uncle Hendrick's house. It's too icy and I can't get home. I need you to tell my parents I'm spending the night at Uncle Hendrick's. Okay?"

There was a pause. "Okay," said Ruthie. She sounded very far away.

"Wait, Ruthie!" said Kit. "One more thing. I . . . I wanted to say I'm sorry. I'm really sorry."

The line got all crackly and Inky started to bark and jump up on Kit, so she couldn't hear if Ruthie said anything or not. Finally, Kit hung up.

❧

The room Kit was supposed to sleep in was as cold as a tomb and about as cheery. It had brown wallpaper. The bed was huge, with a headboard that had wooden gargoyles carved into it. The blankets were mustard-colored and musty-smelling. They were heavy, but somehow they didn't keep Kit warm, even though she pulled them up to her nose. No coal fire had been lit in the fireplace for a long, long time. *If we are evicted from our house, and we have to come and live with Uncle Hendrick, will this be my room?* Kit wondered. She shuddered. *I'd rather live in a dungeon.*

For endless hours, Kit lay stiff and miserable, listening to the ice pelt against the window and the wind rage and the house creak and shift. She thought about all that she was missing at home. By now they would have finished decorating the tree. It probably looked very nice, though most likely Dad wouldn't have put any lights on it. He didn't know they were going to be able to pay the electric bill. He didn't know about Kit's surprise. A lump rose in Kit's throat.

Just then, she heard scratching at her door. Kit hid her head under the covers. But it was no use. The scratching only grew louder, and now Kit heard whimpering, too. She tiptoed across the freezing floor and opened the door a crack. Suddenly, something pushed against it. A dark streak bolted across the floor and leaped up onto her bed. It was Inky. Kit climbed back into bed, and Inky curled up next to her. *This has got to be the worst Christmas Eve anyone has ever had!* Kit thought. *No one deserves a Christmas Eve as lonely as this. Not even Inky.* Kit felt so forlorn, she was actually glad for horrible old Inky's smelly, snuffling company. At least he was warm. After a while, Kit fell asleep.

It seemed as if no time at all had passed before a sound woke her. It was the most peculiar thing. Kit was sure she heard jingle bells. She opened her eyes and realized it was morning. The light in the room was murky because of the heavy curtains drawn shut in front of the window. Kit got up and pulled the curtains open. Suddenly, the room was flooded with dazzling light. The sun, shining on the dripping, melting ice outside, made prisms of light swim and shimmer on the walls. The sound of the jingle bells was louder. Kit looked out the window, squinting because the bright light was so blinding. She blinked. She couldn't believe what she saw outside on the sidewalk.

Ruthie and Ruthie's father were standing next to their big black car, jingling bells and looking up at the house.

"Ho, ho, ho! Merry Christmas!" shouted Ruthie when she saw Kit's face at the window. "We've come to rescue you! Hurry up and come down!"

Kit rose up on her toes in happiness. She banged on the window. "I'll be right there!" she yelled. She'd slept in her clothes, so all she had to do was yank on her shoes, which she did, hopping on one foot and then the other, before she dashed down the stairs. She flung open the door and ran straight to Ruthie. "Oh, Ruthie!" she said. "I've never been so happy to see anyone in my life! Thank you for helping me!"

Ruthie smiled. "That's what friends are for," she said.

Kit smiled, too. *Friends!* she thought happily.

When Uncle Hendrick was ready, Mr. Smithens drove them all—including Inky—to the Kittredges' house. Though most of the ice had melted, the roads were slippery, and it was slow-going up the hill. Mr. Smithens skidded as he turned into the Kittredges' driveway, but he pulled the car as close to the house as possible. The front door flew open.

Mother, Dad, Charlie, and all the boarders poured out calling, "Hurray!" and "Merry Christmas!" and "Kit, we missed you!" When Kit jumped out of the car, everyone tried to hug her at once.

"I'll come back this evening to give you a ride home, sir." Mr. Smithens said to Uncle Hendrick.

Just before she went inside, Kit turned and waved good-bye to Ruthie. "Thanks again! See you later!" she called. "Merry Christmas!"

"Merry Christmas!" Ruthie called back cheerily, waving through the car window.

A merry Christmas it was, too, as merry as any Kit had ever known. Dad surprised Kit with her typewriter, fixed and as good as new, and Charlie gave her a box of typing paper. In the typewriter, there was a piece of paper that said:

```
Fur Kit, Morry Chri tma !
with luvo frum pad and Charlio??
For Kit, Merry Christmas!
with love from Dad and Charlie
```

Mother had a surprise for Kit, too. It was a little black Scottie dog pin. "It was given to me when I was your age," said Mother with a twinkle in her eye. "I thought you might like it. Now that Uncle Hendrick is feeling better, you won't be seeing Inky quite so often."

At the sound of his name, Inky started barking. Kit grinned at Mother. "Thanks, Mother," she said, over Inky's ruckus.

But the best surprise by far was Kit's surprise. Kit waited until she and Mother were alone in the kitchen mixing up a batch of waffles.

"We'll eat next to the tree," said Mother. She smiled a small smile. "I'm sure it'll be as lovely as ever, though I *am* sorry we can't have any lights on the tree this year. It just seemed too extravagant, since we can't pay the electric bill."

"Oh yes we can!" said Kit happily. She handed Mother a handkerchief full of coins. "Here's two dollars and forty cents."

Mother looked at the money in disbelief. "For heaven's sake!" she said. "Where did this come from, Kit?"

*Mother looked at the money in disbelief. "For heaven's sake!" she said.*
*"Where did this come from?"*

"From Uncle Hendrick," said Kit. "I earned it."

Mother laughed aloud. "Kit Kittredge," she said. "There never was a girl like you! Wait till I tell your father. He'll be just as proud of you as I am." She threw her arms around Kit and hugged her close. "I hope you are proud of yourself, too."

Kit was.

At dusk, Ruthie and her father came back. Kit and Ruthie presented the scarves they had knitted to their fathers, who didn't seem to mind that the scarves had no fringe. Then Mr. Smithens drove Uncle Hendrick and Inky home, and Kit walked Ruthie back to her house.

They were quiet for a little while. Then Kit said, almost shyly, "Uncle Hendrick is all better. Would you . . . would you like to go window-shopping tomorrow?"

"Sure!" said Ruthie.

"The little Scottie pin my mother gave me will look really nice on the collar of your red dress," said Kit. "That is, if you don't mind if I borrow it." It was too dark to see Ruthie's face, but Kit could tell that she was smiling. Kit went on to say, "That was awfully nice of you to give the ballet tickets to Miss Hart and her boyfriend and Miss Finney and Mr. Peck."

"We can write about their romantic date in our newspaper," said Ruthie, "now that your dad fixed your typewriter. I bet you'll be glad to be writing again. I bet you missed it while you were at your uncle's."

"Well . . ." said Kit. She hesitated, then she said, "Ruthie, I have sort of a present for you. It isn't store-bought or anything. But I made it for you. I hope you like it." Kit pulled a thick envelope out of her coat pocket and handed it to Ruthie. "Merry Christmas," she said.

Ruthie opened the envelope and took out Stirling's sketchpad. "The Story of Princess Ruthie," she read aloud from the cover. She looked through the pages. Kit had written a story to go with Stirling's sketches of Ruthie as a princess. "Oh, Kit!" said Ruthie. "Thank you! I know I'll love it. No one ever wrote a book for me before. And one about a princess, too!"

63

"She's a generous princess," said Kit. "Just like you. In fact, she *is* you. I was thinking of you the whole time I was writing about her."

"This is kind of funny," said Ruthie. "Wait till you see the present my mom and I made for you." Ruthie took a small package wrapped in tissue paper out of *her* coat pocket and handed it to Kit.

Kit unwrapped it and grinned from ear to ear. Ruthie had given her a doll that looked just like Amelia Earhart! The doll was dressed in a flight cap and jacket and gloves just like the ones Amelia Earhart had worn in the newsreel, and she had the same good-humored, eager smile, too. "Thanks, Ruthie," Kit said. "This is the nicest present you could possibly have given me. You're a good friend."

"You're a good friend, too," said Ruthie. "I can't wait to read my princess story. See you tomorrow!"

"Bye," said Kit. "Merry Christmas!"

Kit watched Ruthie run up the driveway and go into the house. Then she turned around to walk home. When she saw her own house down the street, she gasped in surprise.

"Oh, how *beautiful*," she whispered. While she'd been walking Ruthie home, Dad and Charlie had put the lights on the Christmas tree. The lights were lit, and through the window, they glowed as brightly as jewels. Kit stood in the cold and stared at her family's house, where every happy Christmas of her life had taken place. *This may be the last Christmas we'll have in our house,* she thought, feeling a bittersweet joy. *But it's one I'll never forget. It may even have been the very best Christmas of all.*

Looking
Back
1934

# A PEEK INTO
# THE PAST

*Christmas at a "Hooverville," one of the shacks homeless
people named after President Hoover during the Depression*

Millions of families in the 1930s were like Kit's family—
without jobs, without savings, and at risk of losing their
homes. Others were already homeless. People who struggled
to pay the rent and feed their families had little money to
spare for gifts and holiday preparations. But even during the
hard times of the Great Depression,
Americans found ways to celebrate
Christmas.

Families found creative ways to
get Christmas trees and to decorate
their homes for the holidays. One unemployed father surprised his family
with a tree late on Christmas Eve. He
bargained with a tree seller just before

*Some families decorated for
Christmas with cut-out paper
wreaths or candles.*

*Even a small tree helped make the holidays festive.*

the seller closed for Christmas, and got a tree for 25¢. A Wisconsin girl whose family couldn't afford a Christmas tree was given the school's tree the day school closed for Christmas vacation. But as she dragged the tree home in the snow, the spirit of Christmas moved her to give the tree to another family—one that was even poorer than her own.

Families who had artificial trees, which had become popular in the 1920s, put those up. But many families who had trees could not afford the luxury of electric tree lights. Instead, people decorated their trees with tinsel and ornaments from years past, or with strings of popcorn

*Families and friends gathered to share meals, sing carols, and exchange inexpensive or homemade gifts.*

and cranberries. Even less costly decorations were bright strips of cloth or paper, buttons, and paper chains made of colorful magazine pages.

Those who couldn't afford a tree found other ways to make their homes festive. One family decorated a loaf of bread with white icing and a door, windows, and shutters to make a showy snow-covered cottage.

*A cottage made from a loaf of bread*

Department stores still hired men to play Santa Claus during the Depression, and children still enjoyed visiting Santa. But after the Depression started, what children asked Santa for changed. Many said that they wanted jobs for their dads for Christmas. One girl told Santa she would like a doll, but she knew it wouldn't do any good to ask for one while her father was out of work. When asked by a newspaper reporter what they wanted for Christmas, the men who played Santa Claus had similar requests: "I want a job, a real job."

*Some stores gave special pins to children who visited Santa.*

MERRY CHRISTMAS
HAPPY NEW YEAR

*A girl sharing her Christmas wish list with Santa Claus*

*Those with money to spend on Christmas gifts had lots of choices, as this 1930s department store window shows.*

Some families were not as badly affected by the hard times. For those lucky children, there were plenty of toys and gifts to be seen in store windows and catalogues.

Children enjoyed poring through catalogues, dreaming of special toys. Dolls, toy tea sets, games and puzzles, electric train sets, scooters, sleds, and toy airplanes were popular when Kit was a girl. To encourage people to buy, one catalogue offered a "genuine leather aviator helmet" free with any purchase—something a girl like Kit would have loved!

*Aviator caps were inspired by those worn by pilots Amelia Earhart and Charles Lindbergh.*

*Handmade gifts*

Most people made gifts instead of buying them. Parents often hid old toys in the weeks before Christmas. On Christmas morning, those toys would reappear under the tree—with a fresh coat of paint or with broken parts repaired. People made all sorts of gifts, from mittens and scarves to toys and special foods. One farm family sent a special Christmas package to relatives in St. Louis—a box of home-baked pastries and a freshly killed and prepared chicken. For a family short on cash and food, such a package must have been a wonderful gift!

During the holidays, churches, charities, YMCAs, and even public utilities—such as gas and electric companies—received many

*Old toys got a fresh coat of paint at Christmastime.*

letters from families in need. Charities and individual citizens everywhere worked hard to provide Christmas cheer for the unemployed and needy in their communities. In Kit's hometown of Cincinnati, fire department and post office employees, Girl and Boy Scouts, and even

Dear Sirs,
No one in the family is working and it looks like we'll have a bare Christmas—the first we've ever experienced. Are there families in this city who could afford to send us a few toys? Although we can't pay for them, we can at least pray that heaven will be good to those who sent gifts to us.

*Companies received many letters asking for help at Christmastime. A letter like this was sent by a needy mother with seven children.*

*Many communities joined together to provide Christmas toys and cheer for needy children.*

schools contributed to the Mayor's Christmas Fund so that no Cincinnati family would be in need on Christmas Day. They collected clothing, toys, and baskets of food for a Christmas dinner. People who could afford to attend Cincinnati Symphony Orchestra and Conservatory Choir Christmas programs helped by bringing donations of toys and food to every performance. For millions of needy families facing Christmas during the Depression, such efforts were a wonderful reminder that the spirit of Christmas could survive even the hardest of times.

*Christmas baskets were packed with the makings of a Christmas dinner—and sometimes included a small gift.*

*Giving out Christmas baskets*

# THE BOOKS ABOUT KIT

### MEET KIT • An American Girl
Kit Kittredge and her family get news that
turns their household upside down.

### KIT LEARNS A LESSON • A School Story
It's Thanksgiving, and Kit learns a surprising
lesson about being thankful.

### KIT'S SURPRISE • A Christmas Story
The Kittredges may lose their house.
Can Kit still find a way to make Christmas
merry and bright for her family?

*Coming in September 2001*

## HAPPY BIRTHDAY, KIT! • A Springtime Story

## KIT SAVES THE DAY • A Summer Story

## CHANGES FOR KIT • A Winter Story